LEGO NEXO KNIGHTS™

POWER UP!

WRITTEN BY REBECCA L. SCHMIDT

SCHOLASTIC INC.

ISBN: 978-1-338-05559-7

10 9 8 7 6 5 4 3 2 1   17 18 19 20 21

Printed in the U.S.A.   40

First printing 2017

Statues Attack!

NEXO KNIGHTS hero Clay was hard at work in the Knights' Academy when he got a call from Merlok 2.0. Lance was under attack! Although the NEXO KNIGHTS heroes had taken a break from fighting together, Clay knew it was time for them to get back to work.

Jumping into his Falcon Fighter Blaster, Clay raced toward the Lava Lands Amusement Center. He soon found Lance in full NEXO Power mode, surrounded by statues. But the statues were alive and attacking! The Cloud of Monstrox was there, too. What was he up to?

Clay slid his ship to the ground, taking out two of the statues in the process. "Okay, guys! Let's help Lance!"

Clay and Lance had some backup. Macy, Aaron, and Axl flew in, ready to help.

"We have to find their weak spots!" Clay told the team.

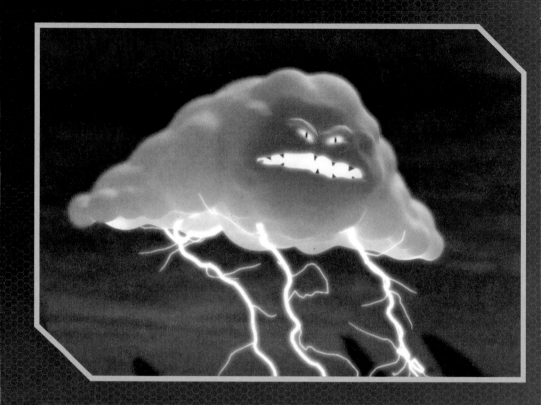

Knights in Trouble!

Lance's powered-up weapon turned a monster back into a statue. But the Cloud of Monstrox had a new power! The knights watched in amazement as the Cloud of Monstrox woke the statue up again with powerful lightning. Without a power-up from Merlok 2.0, the rest of the team's weapons weren't doing anything against the stone monsters. Clay called Ava, who was watching the fight from the Fortrex, for help.

But Ava had bad news. Merlok had already downloaded a NEXO Power to Lance. That meant he couldn't send a power to the rest of the knights!

Lance did his best, but there were just too many stone monsters. Soon, the team was surrounded.

Just then, Jestro burst out of a hidden cave. The Cloud of Monstrox and stone monsters had just been a distraction for Jestro to steal something powerful—a new staff! The knights watched, breathless, as the evil horde of monsters ran away. Clay was sure this wasn't the last they'd see of them.

A New Plan

Clay gathered the team in the Fortrex.

"Monstrox is back. Jestro has joined him. He's leading an army of stone monsters. It's almost too much," Macy said.

"We have to get it together, people!" Clay said. "No matter what we've been doing, we're the NEXO KNIGHTS team. All of Knighton is under threat."

Merlok 2.0 was worried, too. "My concern is the evolving nature of Monstrox's magic. My NEXO Powers can only stun those new monsters, but that cloud can restart them. Ava, we need more power so the knights can take down the stone monsters permanently."

Ava turned to her computer screens. It was time to do some research.

Rune Hunt

Far away in the Knighton countryside, Jestro and the Cloud of Monstrox celebrated their victory over the NEXO KNIGHTS heroes.

"I can feel the evil in this new staff," Jestro said.

"You ain't seen nothing yet," the Cloud of Monstrox said. "We're gonna get something special to really bring it to life."

The Cloud of Monstrox brought Jestro to the Iron Mountains. "In there, some-where, is a Forbidden Power."

"A Forbidden Power?" Jestro asked. He had no idea what that was, but it sounded exciting!

"They won't just give us an edge over those NOTHING Knights; they'll give us the edge over everything," said Monstrox. The evil duo went down a hidden path. Time to power up!

Experimentation!

Meanwhile, Clay and the other knights were fast asleep after a long day of training when—*BAM!*—there was a huge explosion! "Are we under attack?" Clay yelled as the team rushed into the training room ready to fight.

"No, no, no," Merlok 2.0 said. "No attack. It's merely some experimentation!"

Merlok explained his plan to the knights. "Rather than just use one power, why not combine NEXO Powers to give them even more, uh, awesomeness? So I had Robin build the NEXO Power Triangulator to, uh, triangulate NEXO Powers!" the magician said.

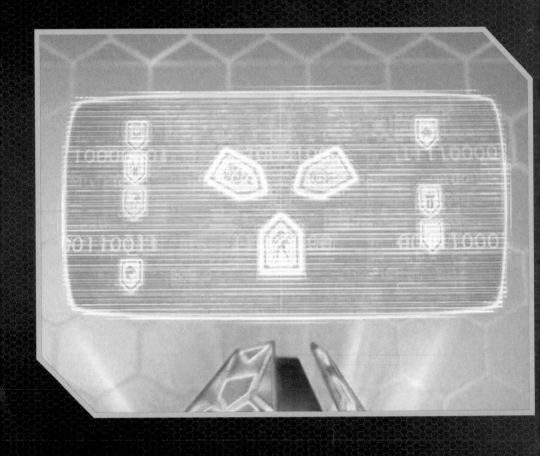

"Combining NEXO Powers? I like the sound of that!" Clay said.

"Let's give it another go!" Ava said, as she pressed a button.

"Oh my, yes!" Merlok 2.0 said. "Funky Fungus! Rolling Fire Ball! Banana Bomb!"

Ava was worried. "Merlok, that Combo is at 2 percent!" There was no way that those powers would combine correctly. But it was too late.

"Funky Rolling Banana Bomb!"

The Triangulator flashed and spun. With a loud *BOOM*, the lights went out. When they came back on, the room's walls were covered with burnt bananas. That wouldn't be much help against Jestro's army.

Obviously, the Triangulator needed some work. Clay just worried that they were running out of time.

Armorville Alive!

Clay was right to worry. Jestro had returned from the Iron Mountains where he had found the Forbidden Power of Relentless Rust and a new monster, the Rogul. They were attacking Armorville!

Jestro raised his staff with a new tablet that contained the Forbidden Power. "Rogul of Relentless Rust, show that you can earn my trust, and turn Armorville into a bust!"

The ghostly Rogul rose up and started to attack the town of Armorville. Everything that he touched turned from polished stone into rust!

"Yes! It works! Now, minions, let's trash this town!" Jestro ordered.

The monsters began to tear the town apart as villagers ran for safety.

The NEXO KNIGHTS heroes soon arrived on the scene. "Leave no stone unturned in defense of this town!" Clay ordered.

"Ack! Give me a moment; that line is making me gag," said Lance.

But the knights didn't have time to banter. There were enemies to face!

The Cloud of Monstrox flew through the town. He was bringing all of Armorville's statues to life! They all started to attack the knights.

"I hit 'em and it barely does anything!" Axl complained.

"I know. Their stone skin is too hard," Macy said.

Clay Gets Hit!

Clay kept being pushed back and back until he hit a statue. He climbed it, hoping to get a good shot at the Cloud of Monstrox.

Just then, Jestro hit Clay with a blast of his rust beam. Clay slammed back into a statue that the Cloud of Monstrox was zapping with a bolt of his lightning.

Clay went flying. For just an instant, he felt very strange. Almost . . . like he was made of stone?

But Clay didn't have time to think about it. There were too many monsters to deal with, and the Rogul was rusting everything—even the knights' armor! Clay picked his sword up and went back to the fight.

"Ava, we're getting overwhelmed!" he called.

Out of Options!

"On it! Maneuvering the Fortrex to support you while we work on a solution," Ava responded. But as the mighty fortress moved closer to the battle, the Rogul appeared and rusted the Fortrex's tracks with a single touch!

"Stopped dead in our tracks," Ava said. "Hey, wizard, we're gonna need some kind of magic to get out of this!"

"Well, then we have to take a chance with the Triangulator! Get ready!" Merlok 2.0 said.

"Okay, knights, point your shields together!" Ava ordered.

Back in the battle, Clay, Lance, and Macy all raised their shields.

"Combo NEXO Power: DOWNLOAD!" Merlok 2.0 cried.

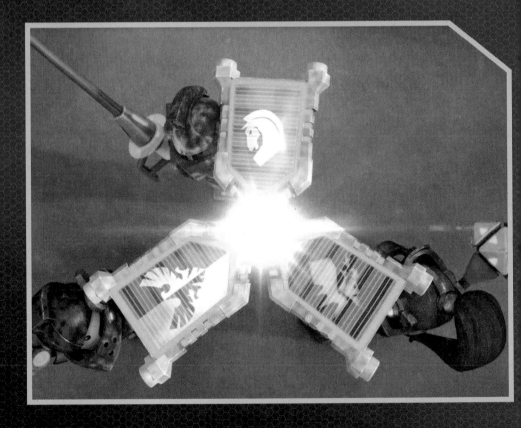

"Magnetize! Rock Ripper! Hawk Caller!" Merlok said. The Triangulator whirled. Clay held his breath. The knights needed this Combo Power to work if they had any hope of defeating Jestro's horde of monsters.

"Combo NEXO Power: Magnetic Rocky Hawk!" Merlok 2.0 declared.

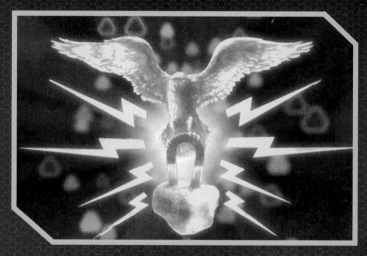

Combo NEXO Power!

Clay's, Macy's, and Lance's armor and weapons transformed as the power downloaded. It had worked! Two stone monsters ran up to him, but Clay slammed down his sword. A fiery blast shot out, shattering a group of stone monsters.

"Whoa! That Combo Power seems to do the trick," Clay said.

"We gotta get outta here before they use that wacky new power on us!" the Cloud of Monstrox said.

"No fair! They're not supposed to adjust; they're supposed to be defeated!" Jestro said.

"Yeah, well, we adjust, they adjust . . . it's a whole thing. Let's scram!" the Cloud of Monstrox said. Jestro and the Cloud of Monstrox ran for it as the knights destroyed the last of the Stone Monsters.

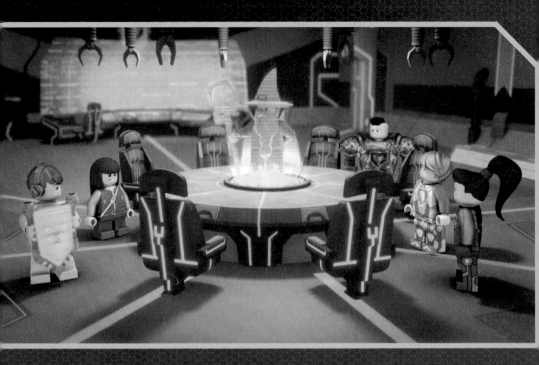

Clay in Trouble

Later that day, the knights gathered for a meeting.
"Now we can use a Combo NEXO Power every time to beat Jestro," Macy said.

"Whoa, hey, slow down," Ava said. It wasn't going to be as easy as all the knights thought. "On any given day, the Combo NEXO Power will depend on a number of factors: environmental, power employed against rating, combo-transfer properties . . ."

"So you're sayin' that today . . ." Axl said, starting to get worried.

"We got pretty, pretty lucky," Ava replied.

Merlok 2.0 realized that a member of the team was missing. Where was Clay?

The wizard found the team leader practicing in the training room. "Clay, my boy, you're not reveling in your victory with your cohorts?" he asked.

"No, Merlok. Something happened to me out there. I can't explain it. The Cloud of Monstrox zapped a statue I was touching and, now, well, I just don't feel right."

   Merlok raised his staff above Clay,
performing a digital scan of him. "Oh,
my, let's see," Merlok said.
   "What is it?" Clay asked.
   "Some very dark magic indeed is
at work here. Something ancient that
I haven't seen in a long, long time. I
will work on a solution, so don't worry,"
Merlok said.

Clay hoped Merlok was right. He knew that, even with the new Combo NEXO Powers, Jestro, the Cloud of Monstrox, and the Forbidden Powers were still a threat. Clay knew that, together, the NEXO KNIGHTS team would be ready for anything!